Romeo and Juliet

Sweet Cherry
Publishing

Published by Sweet Cherry Publishing Limited
Unit E, Vulcan Business Complex,
Vulcan Road,
Leicester, LE5 3EB,
United Kingdom

First published in the UK in 2012
ISBN: 978-1-78226-012-7

©Macaw Books

Title: Romeo and Juliet

Text & Illustration by Macaw Books 2012

www.sweetcherrypublishing.com

Printed in India by Ajanta Offset and Packagings Limited

About *Shakespeare*

William Shakespeare, regarded as the greatest writer in the English language, was born in Stratford-upon-Avon in Warwickshire, England (around 23 April 1564). He was the third of eight children born to John and Mary Shakespeare.

Shakespeare was a poet, playwright and dramatist. He is often known as England's national poet and the 'Bard of Avon'. Thirty-eight plays, one hundred and fifty-four sonnets, two long narrative poems and several other poems are attributed to him. Shakespeare's plays have been translated into every major existent language and are performed more often than those of any other playwright.

Romeo: He is born into the house of Montague. He falls in love with Juliet, a Capulet, and secretly marries her. He is intelligent, impulsive, immature and a devoted friend. He is caught up in a violent feud between his family and the Capulets.

Juliet: She is the only child of the Capulets. She is beautiful and obedient. She appears immature, but gradually becomes more mature and shows tremendous courage as the play progresses.

Friar Lawrence: He is kind and always ready with a plan. He is friend to both Romeo and Juliet,

and he marries them in secret. He helps Romeo flee, and also has knowledge about various mystical potions and herbs.

Paris: He is a suitor to Juliet and is preferred by the Capulets. He is wealthy and handsome, but self-absorbed.

Romeo and Juliet

Many years ago in Verona, Italy, there lived two noble families who were engaged in a bitter feud: the Montagues and the Capulets. From the masters of the house to the servants, they would all get into terrible fights with each other.

Montague had only one son, Romeo, and Capulet was similarly blessed with one daughter, Juliet.

One day, the servants from the Capulet family were walking by when they saw that two servants from the Montague household were coming their way. So, one of the Capulet servants told his friend that he would show his thumb to the Montague servants, which would infuriate them.

Needless to say, the Montague
servants did not take the showing
of the thumb lightly and soon
they were all engaged in a fight
in the middle of the street.

Benvolio, Romeo's cousin,
on seeing the servants fighting,
went over and tried to stop
them. But Tybalt, a member

of the Capulet household, who
was passing, tried to pick a fight
with him. Benvolio explained,
"I just want to make peace."
To which Tybalt replied curtly,
"Talk of peace! I hate the
word as I hate all Montagues!
Here, take this … coward!"

12

But before Tybalt could attack Benvolio, officers of Prince Escalus, the ruler of Verona, intervened and stopped the two families fighting. Prince Escalus was getting rather tired of these frequent bloodbaths on his streets and he immediately issued a declaration that if he ever caught either family involved in a fight again, he would make sure they paid with their lives. So for a while, both families managed to live with each other in peace.

One day, Benvolio found
Romeo looking rather pale and
sad. He knew that his cousin
was troubled by the woman
of his dreams, Rosaline, who
was not interested in him at
all. Benvolio tried his best to
get Romeo to forget about
her, but he refused to listen.

Meanwhile, in another part of the town, Lord Capulet was making arrangements for a party at his house. He had invited, among other guests, a young man by the name of Paris, who was in love with his daughter, Juliet.

He handed the list to one of his servants and asked him to invite all the people mentioned on that piece of paper. However, Capulet did not realise that his servant was illiterate.

Not knowing what to do, the servant walked aimlessly down the road, when suddenly,

he saw two men approaching. He
asked them if they could tell him
what was written on the piece of
paper so that he could complete
his task as soon as possible.
Romeo and Benvolio saw that
it was a list of all the invitees to
Capulet's party, and Benvolio
had an idea. After they explained

the task to the servant and he was
gone, Benvolio turned to Romeo
and said that they should go to
the party and meet some ladies.
Benvolio was confident that once
Romeo had met someone else, he
would soon forget about Rosaline.

At first, Romeo was not
sure whether they should go,
considering the bitter animosity

between the two families. But
Benvolio, along with their friend,
Mercutio, was able to convince
Romeo, telling him that since it
was a masquerade party, no one
would know their true identities.

At the party, Romeo
saw Juliet for the first time.

Her father had brought her
along so that she could spend
some time with Paris and get
to know him. Romeo soon
forgot about Rosaline and
fell in love with Juliet.

Tybalt, who was also at the
party, recognised Romeo and

was furious that a Montague had come into his house. He wanted to attack and kill Romeo at once. Seeing Tybalt dash towards one of his guests, Lord Capulet came before him and asked him what he was up to. On being told that Romeo had come to the party uninvited, Capulet merely told

Tybalt to restrain himself. He commented that Romeo had not misbehaved in any way and he did not want any blood spilt in his house. Tybalt was not willing to listen to reason, but Capulet managed to hold him back.

Meanwhile, Romeo wanted to know who the fair maiden was that had captured his heart. Slowly he moved towards Juliet and managed to pull her away from the crowd. But as he started talking to her, Juliet's maid arrived and informed her that her mother was looking

for her. Romeo, who still did
not know Juliet's true identity,
asked the maid who her mother
was, to which she replied, "Her
mother is the lady of the house."

Romeo was crestfallen. He
exclaimed to himself, "She is a
Capulet!" Unable to bear the
weight of this knowledge, he
drifted away from the party.

Juliet, seeing Romeo leave, asked
her maid who the young man
was, because she had fallen in

love with him. On being told that he was a Montague, the only son of her great enemy, she cried, "My only love has sprung from my only hate!"

Unable to stay away from Juliet, Romeo climbed the wall of the orchard at the back of

the Capulet house. As he stood thinking about his newfound love, he saw her on the balcony. Soon, he heard her say, "O Romeo, Romeo! Why do you have to be Romeo? O, be of some other name! What is in a name? That which we call a rose, by any other name would smell as sweet!"

Romeo now knew that Juliet had fallen in love with him, and unable to restrain himself any longer, he came out of the bushes and said, "Call me Love, or by any other name. Henceforth I shall never be Romeo again!"

They talked through the
night, expressing their love
for each other, and soon they
realised they would not be able
to live without each other. But
time was ticking and dawn was
fast approaching. If Romeo
were found, he would surely be

33

killed, so they bade farewell, promising to meet again.

Romeo could not contain his excitement and immediately went to Friar Lawrence's chambers to make arrangements for his marriage to Juliet.

At the same time, Mercutio
called on Benvolio to find out if
Romeo had returned home the
previous night. He had not, and
Mercutio was told that Tybalt
had left a message for Romeo,
challenging him to a duel.

Benvolio and Mercutio set off in search of Romeo.

After leaving Friar Lawrence's chambers, Romeo went to meet Juliet's maid. He told her that she must tell Juliet to go to Friar Lawrence's church that afternoon. Juliet's maid hurried back to convey Romeo's message, and as planned, Romeo and Juliet got married that same day.

It was late in the evening when Benvolio and Mercutio finally found Romeo walking towards them, beaming from ear to ear. They asked him where he

38

had been all day, but suddenly,
Tybalt came on the scene and
wanted to exchange blows with
Romeo. But now that he was
married to Tybalt's cousin,
Juliet, Romeo had no intention
of getting into a fight with him.
But Mercutio, not knowing the
truth, thought that Romeo was

afraid to fight the evil Capulet,
so drew his own sword and
challenged Tybalt to a duel.
Romeo tried desperately to stop
them, but in the confusion,
Tybalt thrust his sword and
stabbed Mercutio to death.

Romeo was enraged by what
had happened. He told Tybalt,
"Either you, or me, or both, must
go with Mercutio." And they

started to fight. After some time,
Romeo killed Tybalt. Benvolio
urged him to run away, as the

prince's men would surely kill him if he were found.

When the prince and his officials arrived at the scene of the crime, Benvolio, who was the only witness, was forced to tell them what had happened. The prince was confused, as he knew that Romeo had only killed Tybalt because Tybalt had killed Mercutio. Therefore, he did not send Romeo to the gallows, but declared that he

should be banished from the city of Verona immediately.

Romeo was hiding in Friar Lawrence's chambers when he was brought the news. Friar Lawrence advised him to leave for Mantua until he could announce his marriage to Juliet, when, upon seeking the prince's forgiveness, he could return to Verona.

Meanwhile, Lord Capulet
was making arrangements for
Juliet's marriage to Paris in three
days' time. Juliet tried to resist,
citing Tybalt's death as a cause
for mourning, not a celebration,
but her pleas fell on deaf ears.

Juliet was heartbroken,
as Romeo had already left
for Mantua. Faced with such
trouble, she decided to pay Friar
Lawrence a visit, believing he was
the only man who could help her.

Friar Lawrence listened and
felt that there was only one way

he could help her. He asked her to go home and give her consent to marry Paris, but he gave her a vial containing a special liquid which, once consumed, would make people believe she was

dead. So, the next morning,
when her family members found
her, they would have to bury
her in the ancient vault where
all the Capulets lay. Meanwhile,
Friar Lawrence would inform
Romeo, who would come and
take her away to Mantua, where

they could lead a happy married
life without anyone knowing.

Juliet agreed to Friar
Lawrence's proposal. She went
home and told her father that
she was willing to marry Paris.
Before she went to bed, she
had second thoughts about
consuming the special liquid

the Friar had given her. What if it was poison? What if Romeo arrived too late and she awoke? Perhaps she would suffocate in the vault and die! But her love for Romeo made her overcome her fears and she drank the entire contents of the bottle.

As expected, the next morning her maid found her dead. The Capulet household was shocked at her sudden demise, and just as Friar Lawrence predicted, she was laid to rest with all the other Capulets in their ancient vault.

Meanwhile, Friar Lawrence had sent his friend, Friar John, to Mantua with the message for Romeo. However, before Friar John could reach him, the unfortunate news about Juliet had spread far and wide, also reaching her beloved Romeo.

Romeo was moved to tears at the news and decided to return to Verona that very night. But before leaving, he acquired some poison for himself.

When Friar John returned and told Friar Lawrence about Romeo's disappearance

from Mantua, the Friar knew
that there was great danger
lurking that night. He knew
that Romeo would not take
the news of his beloved Juliet
lightly and there was no telling

what he might do to himself.
He therefore decided to bring
Juliet to his own chambers until
Romeo could be found.

That night, Paris also decided
to pay his respects to Juliet at

her grave. As he was leaving, he saw Romeo enter the vault. He thought Romeo had come to degrade the bodies of Tybalt and

Juliet, and enraged, he drew his sword and leapt at Romeo. But Romeo was not in the right state of mind and, within a few minutes, he had slain Paris.

At Paris' dying request, Romeo carried his body into the grave so that he could lie with Juliet. Finally, Romeo got to see Juliet again. The Friar's liquid had indeed proved quite effective, for though it was nearly time for Juliet to wake up from her slumber, she still

appeared dead to Romeo. With
one parting kiss for his beloved
wife, Romeo stood and drank
the poison he had brought from
Mantua. Within a few moments,
he lay next to Juliet, dead.

Just as Romeo breathed
his last, Friar Lawrence arrived

to find that he was too late. At that moment, Juliet woke up and realised what had happened. Friar Lawrence told her that she should leave with him, but she was in no mood to listen. She was devastated to see Romeo lying there dead before her, and

decided that without him she had no reason to live. Taking Romeo's dagger, she stabbed herself and fell onto Romeo, dead.

When the watchman discovered what had happened, both families were asked to gather in the vault. The prince declared that the two young lovers had died because of their families' erring ways, and it dawned on them how futile their enmity had been, taking from them their own children.

Capulet took Montague's hand in his and they ended their feud once and for all, deciding to erect statues to commemorate Romeo and Juliet's love for each other.